This book belongs to

....

I Spy with My Little Eye

TACO TRUCK
SNACK & FIND

Written by Rubie Crowe
Illustrated by Josh Cleland

cottage door press®

Folks say the Truckin' Taco has the best tacos around, and every day I track the truck around the busy town.

The busy bees who run the Honey in a Hurry truck are all over town. Can you find them in every scene?

I need a letter mailed quickly! Where is the mail carrier?

BURGERS

CHEESE QUACKERS

CITY SPRINKLES

FARMER'S MARKET

Count 10 food trucks.

Find 3 umbrellas.

STADIUM

BIG SAMMY'S

THE GOLDEN NUGGET

CAFÉ

BOOKS

VEGGIE DOGS

TACOS

Find the tall slide.

Oh my, it's such a windy day.
Spot a balloon that got away.

I've come so close so many times, but still I've had no luck,
to try a tasty taco from the Truckin' Taco truck!

At the summer City Marathon, I was just across the street.
Close enough to catch a whiff, but still too far to eat!

I spy with my little eye a number
that is twice 24 minus 11.
Who is number 37?

This famous racing duo doesn't
have time to spare. Where do
you see the tortoise and hare?

I spy with my little eye 6 fluttering butterflies, each a color of the rainbow.

Where is the kid wearing butterfly wings?

DONUT

At the Bumblebee Street Fair, I couldn't find my money. It fell out of my pocket and got stuck in sticky honey.

CITY SPRINKLES

TACO

Did you know that a beehive is a hairstyle, too? Can you spot someone with a twisty beehive hairdo?

Find a fabulous pair of flowery platform shoes.

Find 2 matching flower hats.

Special: FROSTING TACOS

TACOS

Special
Banana
TACOS

Octopi like tacos, too. Can you spot one who has a few?

Splitzville

Where is the sandcastle with 2 towers and a moat?

FROSTY CONE

I really thought "third time's the charm" at Sand Dollar Beach,
but the waves kept me at bay and the tacos out of reach.

Find 2 friends sharing
the twin ice pop.

I spy with my little eye
6 silver starfish.

He fell asleep while getting tanned and his
kids buried him in the sand! Can you spot him?

TACOS

Special:
KALE-FREE TACOS

Yuck! I spy someone who doesn't know about the five-second rule.

Find 4 green tote bags.

This shopper has been here for hours! Her arms are filled with bread and flowers. Can you find her?

At the farmer's market, I joined the wrong line by mistake.
And instead of crunchy tacos, at the end were kale shakes!

These fireworks are pretty good. Can you spot one that's shaped like food?

PIE-FIVE!

BIG SAMMY'S

I spy with my little eye the missing slice of chocolate pie.

Find a super tall sandwich.

Count 5 sparklers.

FRY GUY

VEGGIE-DOGS

TACOS

Find the 3-foot-long veggie dog.

A-tisket, a-tasket, can you spot the purple picnic basket?

I got distracted by the fireworks on Independence Day.
While I was staring at the sky, the taco truck drove away!

The crowd at Concert in the Park seemed so kind and polite,
I'm not sure how the taco line became a funny food fight!

This musician has no more toots to toot.
Where do you see their missing flute?

Caught up in the food tsunami,
find 3 flying pink salami.

CHEESE & QUACKERS

TACOS

Special: Flying TACOS

What got stuck in the tuba?

Find a penny, pick it up, and all the day you'll have good luck. Can you find 6 more?

I spy with my little eye a goat who got hit with a pie. Can you spot him, too?

WHIP Cream

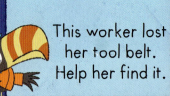
This worker lost her tool belt. Help her find it.

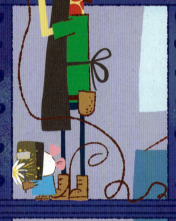

That's a little too much crunch. Can you spy someone who burned their lunch?

Find 10 orange hard hats.

The food trucks' food is way less boring. Find 5 lunch boxes the workers are ignoring.

PEPE RONI'S PIZZA

It's lunchtime at the jobsite. Find the high-up worker taking a bite.

Once at the construction site,
I almost had my chance.
But then I stepped in wet cement
and couldn't move my pants.

Can you escape the corn maze?

Spy 6 spooky specters.

At the scary Scarecrow Fest, I kind of lost my way.
I saw corncobs and baked potatoes. No tacos today!

HOT POTATO

Apple cider, candy apples, and apple pie, oh my! Can you find 1 regular apple?

GOBS of COBS

There sure are lots of carved pumpkins. Can you find the jack-o'-lantern twins?

I thought birds were afraid of scarecrows. Can you spot one posing for photos?

TACO-1

I waited patiently for hours at the Hometown Tailgate.
They left a sign they'd be right back, but then it got so late.

GO Butterflies

These superfans are living the dream. Can you find 6 friends who spell "GO TEAM"?

STADIUM

TACOS

Be RIGHT BACK

BURGERS

I spy with my little eye the biggest fan of #25.

Ants love tailgating, too. Can you spot the tiny barbecue?

Can you count 3 footballs?

This fan's burger is too plain. Can you help them find ketchup, mustard, pickles, and tomato?

One day I tried a taco from a different taco truck.
I thought, really, how bad could it be?

THE ORIGINAL
PICKLE ON A ST

People are flying lots of flags today.
Can you spot the green one?

Spaghetti on WHEELS

FOOD FEST

The ticket roll has
rolled away! Can you
follow the trail to track
down the spool?

TICKETS

Special: 100% MOLD FREE

This guy knows the best, from burgers to fries. Can you spot the clipboard-holding judge in disguise?

Where is the green bird?

I spy with my little eye 3 blue ribbons.

THE GOLDEN NUGGET

JUNKYARD TACOS

77% MOLD FREE

You have no idea. Yuck!

FINALLY! I'm next in line! Today, without a doubt I'll finally get my taco!

Can you see where a pizza is being delivered?

ZA SPOT

INSTRUMENT REPAIR SHOP

Café

What's for lunch? The skunks couldn't agree. What did they get? Can you spot all 3?

LEMONADE

fresh SQUEEZED

A sour lemon doesn't want to be squeezed today. Can you find the one that rolled away?

I spy with my little eye a pair of red cowboy boots.

TACOS

SOLD OUT

Special: 2 for 1

OH NO!
They're all
SOLD OUT???

"Excuse me, but I have an extra taco. Would you like…"

YESSSS!!

Crunchy, cheesy, spicy ... wow, it really is so great!
Thumbs up, five stars, excellent!
Definitely worth the wait!

Count 12 empty taco shells.